JUST THURSDAY

Look for more of
doug & mike's Strange Kid Chronicles:

#1 Mighty Monday Madness

#2 Tuna Fish Tuesday

#3 Wisenheimer Wednesday

Coming soon to a bookstore near you:

#5 Fateful Friday

. . . but don't look for anything else yet because
we've only had time to do one week's worth.

DOUG & MIKE'S
STRANGE KID
CHRONICLES

JUST THURSDAY

AN
APPLE
PAPERBACK

SCHOLASTIC INC.
New York Toronto London Auckland Sydney

ISBN 0-590-05957-2

12 11 10 9 8 7 6 5 4 3 2 1   8 9/9 0 1 2 3/0

Printed in the U.S.A.   40
First Scholastic printing, October 1998

dedicated to my Grampa Fred

Douglas TenNapel is a California native who likes to write stories and draw pictures. This book is the fourth children's book he has written. Douglas has a pet emperor scorpion named Mary-Kate.

dedicated to Dad and Mom

Michael Koelsch was born in Massachusetts but has lived in California long enough to be mistaken for a native. He only wears shorts and T-shirts. Mike has no pets at this time, only because his two girls are enough at the moment.

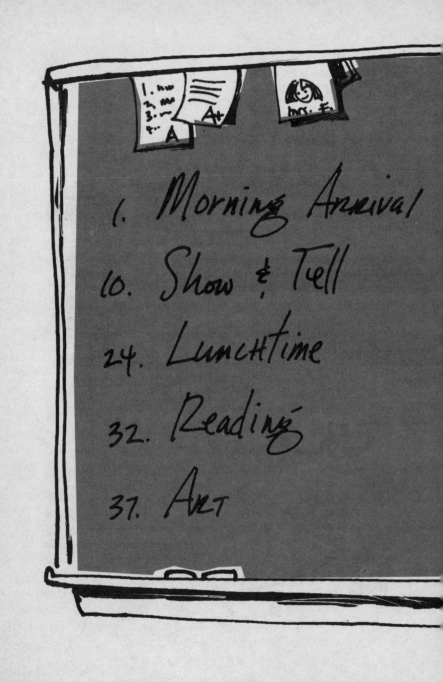

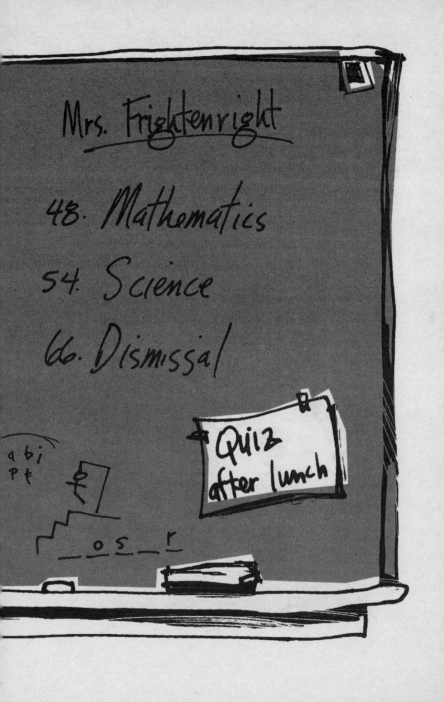

Good Golly Gosh!

Once again, Mrs. Frightenright's insane class is having some strange problems! At least the week is past the halfway point so perhaps they'll make it to the weekend after all. But at this school, you can't count on it!

That nasty Principal Prickly-Pear is up to some*thing!* And you can bet that something is not a good thing. So we won't turn our backs on him . . . will we?! Read on and behold the mysteries that Thursday contains for Mrs. Frightenright's class!

Pretty cool . . . Very tempting . . .
I dare you not to turn the page.

I DARE YOU!

Boy, that was easy. We didn't even have to
DOUBLE DOG DARE YOU!

MORNING ARRIVAL

Mikey Mold stood outside of Doug O'Dork's house and kept checking his watch every thirty seconds. Mikey looked up at Doug's bedroom window and yelled, "Hey! Idiot! Get your pea brain down here or you'll make us late for school AGAIN!"

1

The curtains cracked open and Doug O'Dork looked out the window with his hair all messed up. Doug glanced down at his watch and realized that he must have slept through his alarm clock! He yelled down to Mikey Mold,

"Hold on! I'll be down in two seconds!"

Mikey Mold looked down at his watch and counted out loud, "One Mississippi, two Mississippi."

Mikey heard a voice coming from behind him. "Okay, I'm ready!"

Mikey turned around and saw that it was Doug O'Dork. "That's pretty fast," Mikey said. "Are you sure you're ready to go to school?!"

Doug O'Dork replied, "Yeah, man, I got my pimiento loaf sandwich for lunch and everything."

Just as they turned to walk to school, a big yellow schoolbus drove by and stopped at a big red stop sign, right in front of Doug's big house. The students inside the packed bus were laughing hard. Doug looked up at them and said, "Man, I wonder what they're all laughing at?!"

Doug O'Dork found an open bus win-

dow and asked, "Hey, what are you guys laughing at?"

One of the kids yelled back at Doug,

"You aren't wearing any clothes!"

Doug slowly looked down and realized that he was naked as a jaybird, standing on the sidewalk. Mikey instantly laughed as loud as he could. "Man, I was gonna see if I could get you all the way to school like that!"

Doug O'Dork broke the world record for the ten-meter dash back to his house. He put on some clothes and ran back out to meet Mikey. The boys walked to school and from the exact second they arrived, Doug just turned red in the face every time one of those kids on the bus came up to him, announcing, "I liked the invisible clothes you were wearing this morning." Another shouted, "Nice birthday suit! Next time try wearing it on your birthday!"

But the most popular was probably,

"Hey, freckle-butt!"

Mikey Mold had to drag Doug O'Dork up to the line outside of Mrs. Frightenright's class. The rest of the class was lined up and unusually silent. They were quietly listening to the argument Mrs. Frightenright and Principal Prickly-Pear were having on the other side of the door.

Principal Prickly-Pear said, "You will teach the class the way I tell you to or you will lose your job!"

Mrs. Frightenright said, "But making the students pledge allegiance to you every morning is insane!"

He yelled back, "The students must learn that I am their leader!"

Mrs. Frightenright stopped, lowered her voice, and said, "With all due respect, Principal Prickly-Pear, will you please leave this classroom so I can teach MY class?!"

Principal Prickly-Pear opened the door and Big Mouth Moira fell into the room because she was leaning her ear so hard against the door. Principal Prickly-Pear looked down at her and pointed a finger back at Mrs. Frightenright and said, "You see? This is the kind of disrespect we cannot allow!"

Principal Prickly-Pear put on a big fake smile and spoke sweetly to the other students in line, "Good morning, class! Come in. Have a good day!" As he walked away, Doug O'Dork noticed that a red octopus tentacle was hanging out of the sleeve of his tacky orange plaid suit. The class stormed into Mrs. Frightenright's room, hung up their coats, and got out their books.

Doug O'Dork sat in his chair and leaned back against the desk behind him to whisper to his pal Mikey Mold. Doug whispered for about a minute before he realized that Mikey wasn't there! He was whispering into thin air. Doug rolled his eyes and spoke under his breath, "Not again!"

Doug O'Dork got up, walked across the classroom to the door, and opened it. There stood Mikey Mold, who just plain forgot to walk into the classroom with the rest of the students. Mikey was crying, wondering where all of his classmates had gone. Doug yelled, "Mikey! Get in here!"

Mikey walked into the class and said, "Man, I was wondering why I was getting so cold!"

Mrs. Frightenright took attendance and straightened out the papers on her desk. She looked up at the smiling faces of her class and asked, "Are we ready for show-and-tell?"

The class spoke simultaneously,
"We're ready for show-and-tell,
Mrs. Frightenright!"

"Doug O'Dork, would you
like to go first today?" Mrs.
Frightenright asked.

Mikey Mold started laugh-
ing and said, "Doug already
played show-and-tell this morn-

ing outside his house!"

Mrs Frightenright turned to Mikey Mold. "I see **you** would rather share with the class . . . wouldn't you, Mikey?"

Mikey Mold broke out in a cold sweat and dragged himself to the front of the class. "Um, I don't have anything to show so I'd like to tell a story instead. Is that okay, Mrs. Frightenright?"

She nodded.

Mikey Mold cleared his throat and said, "Here is my story:

Onceuponatimetherewasagreat bigsharkthatlovedtoeatevery one.Onedayitdevouredeveryone inthewholeworld.
TheEnd!"

Mikey ran back to his desk and wiped the sweat off his forehead with his T-shirt.

Mrs. Frightenright said, "That gets the award for the shortest show-and-tell sharing in the history of my class.

"I'm looking for someone else to share!" Mrs. Frightenright continued. A bunch of kids raised their hands. Mrs. Frightenright said, "I'm looking for a certain someone who loves to talk to spiders!"

Spider Speaking Spencer smiled as he walked up to the front of the class. He carried a dirty shoe box cradled under one arm. "I brought the most amazing, fantastic thing you have ever seen!" he said.

The class leaned forward and set their gaze on the mysterious box.

"What is it?" Jared grunted.

"Is it an animal?" Mikey Mold asked.

"Is it enough candy for the whole class?" Truman asked.

"Am I in that box?" Weird Ellis asked.

Everyone thought for a second, then turned to Ellis and looked at him like he was crazy.

Spencer waited for it to be quiet and then said, "I found it in a graveyard."

"Oooooh!" the class gasped excitedly.

Spencer reached down and unfastened the twine holding the box shut. The twine released its grasp on the box and fell to the

floor. He slowly lifted the lid and peeked inside. Snapping the lid shut, he said teasingly, "You're going to like this!"

The class yelled in unison,

"Get on with it, man!"

Just then, a low rumble could be heard from the ground under the classroom. Mrs. Frightenright pointed and yelled, "OH, MY!!! Look at Fang's cage!"

Fang was the class hamster that had been eaten by a werewolf earlier in the week. After Fang's departure from this world, Mrs. Frightenright had decided to keep his empty cage as a memorial to the world's most ferocious hamster. The cage, for the most part, had remained quiet . . . until now. The whole cage shook and the little hamster wheel spun about a hundred miles an hour all by itself. Then the little water bottle started to empty itself and the pine shavings on the chicken-wire floor crunched and flitted about.

Suddenly a green mist appeared in the cage. And you would not believe it unless you saw it . . . the mist started to form into a little green hamster with giant sickle-like teeth! Mikey Mold and Doug O'Dork held each other and trembled like Jell-O in an earthquake. Mikey Mold screamed,

Doug said, "I remember that! Ha! Ha! Fang couldn't bite us for the whole day, his mouth was stuck so tight!"

Mikey boasted, "Yeah, it was pretty funny."

But then, in a frightful monster movie sort of way, Fang's eyes glowed red as he spoke. "Miiiiiikey Mold. I have come back for you!"

Mikey screamed in terror as the green ghost of Fang grew bigger, busting out of his cage. Fang stopped growing after he was about eight feet tall. There he was . . . a gigantic, green, hamster ghost. Fang suddenly lifted his feet off the ground and floated toward poor Mikey!

"Help! He's gonna bite me!" Mikey screamed.

Doug O'Dork piped in, "Don't be silly. He won't bite you . . ."

This relaxed Mikey a bit.

Doug added, ". . . He's gonna swallow you whole and you will slowly digest in his ghostly stomach!"

Mikey's eyes rolled back in his head.

Doug tried to comfort Mikey. "Maybe we'll still see you in his stomach since Fang's transparent!"

Mikey passed out.

"He's getting even bigger!" Mrs. Frightenright screamed.

Weird Ellis knew a lot about specters and hamster ghosts. He spent one full year at the university doing advanced hamster ghost studies. Ellis figured he should study something that was practical to use in his day-to-day life, so he took the class instead of math. He stood up and spoke to the class with authority, "The hamster is growing off of our fear!"

 Big Mouth Moira spoke through chattering teeth, "How can we keep from reacting to this hopeless terror set before us?!"

"We must make him shrink by being happy!" said Ellis.

Truman held up his hands in fear. "I'm completely terrified! How can I be happy that Fang's about to eat Mikey Mold, possibly splattering his innards all over the classroom?!"

"Now, knock that off!" Mikey screamed.

Big Mouth Moira got an idea. "Let's tell jokes!"

"Good idea!" Mrs. Frightenright said. "Everyone think of a funny joke. Then tell it to the class."

Everyone concentrated, but they were so scared and Fang's ghost was growing so big that the class could only think of the hamster eating them.

Big Mouth Moira said, "Hey, everybody! I've got a joke!"

The class screamed in unison, "Tell us, man! Tell us!"

Moira asked, "What's brown and green and sits in the shavings of Fang's hamster cage?"

"What?" the class screamed.

Moira answered, "*Us*, after we've been eaten and digested by Fang!"

The class moaned as Fang grew so big that he touched the ceiling. Fang stood over poor Mikey Mold, who was on the floor with his eyes closed. The giant hamster opened his mouth and was about to eat poor Mikey when Spencer jumped right between them. Fang intended to close his mighty jaws around Spencer's head, but instead, he missed and bit into Spider Speaking Spencer's old show-and-tell shoe box! The hamster swallowed the shoe box in one mighty gulp. Spencer, bewildered, gaped at the empty space between his hands, now void of any show-and-tell box.

Big Mouth Moira shouted out, "Spencer, before we all get eaten up by Fang

and become nothing but digested body parts, I have one last request . . . I must know what the heck was in that stupid box anyways! I admit that curiosity has gotten the better of me!!!"

"Ummm . . ." Spencer scratched his head. "I can't remember! I'm so scared that I forgot!"

Mrs. Frightenright scowled. "You built up our curiosity over this incredible thing in that old shoe box and now that Fang ate it, you can't remember? You mean we'll never know what was in that box?!"

Spencer bowed his head. "I'm sorry, Mrs. Frightenright, but I can't remember."

Suddenly Mrs. Frightenright burst into laughter. "That's the funniest thing I've ever heard!"

The whole classroom erupted with laughter. They laughed so hard that Fang's ghost began to shrink.

"Keep laughing, everybody!" Weird Ellis yelled as tears came out of his eyes from chuckling so hard.

Fang's ghost got a worried look on his face as he continued to shrivel up. He got smaller and smaller until he finally disappeared.

When everyone settled down, Jared raised his hand and requested, "Let's all be silent and let Spencer put on his thinking cap. Maybe then he'll remember what he brought in for show-and-tell."

A silence fell over the classroom as they watched Spencer try to remember what was in the shoe box. Spider Speaking Spencer never did remember what was in that old shoe box, but Mrs. Frightenright knew. It was a lifesaver.

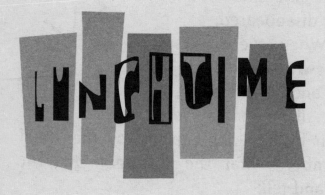

LUNCHTIME

Did you hear that? Just now . . . that's right! Somebody just let out a stinky, juicy burp. That was Barry. If you hear a burp and can't figure out where it came from, it's probably from Barry.

You might be asking yourself, "On a scale of one to ten,

ten being the highest, how does Barry rank as a burper?" He's an eleven!!! It's true! Barry is such an amazing burper that he can make almost any noise he wants with his belch. He can burp the entire alphabet with no problem. If he really wanted to show off, he would burp-speak the whole periodic table (ask your teacher) in less than fifteen seconds.

But Barry's best burping stories happened one summer when Barry went camping with his friends. No one wanted to sleep in a tent with him because of the burp thing, so he slept in a tent all by himself. That night a bunch of bears came down to the campsite. Their mission was to eat as many unsuspecting kids as

they could get their slimy, fat, furry paws on. When the bears got to Barry's tent, they opened the zipper to the door flap. Just when a giant black bear was about to step inside to have a Barry Burger, Barry, in his sleep, let out the hugest, loudest burp ever. The giant black bear jumped back in fright and said to the dumb brown bear, "Hey, man! Did you hear that?"

"What?" the dumb brown bear asked.

"I heard a great big bear roar from inside this here tent," the giant black bear responded. "Dude, I don't want any trouble tonight. My wife thinks I'm out picking berries," he added.

The black bear turned his back on Barry's tent and said, "I'm cool, I'm cool," as his cocky strut instantly turned into a cowardly sprint. "I'm outta here!" he whimpered.

So the bears ran off scared, leaving Barry sleeping in his tent.

So his loud burps were widely accepted by his friends for a while, even in the classroom. Barry could burp so loud that it even disrupted classrooms in other countries. The teachers of those classrooms in other countries didn't like it at all. Barry's friends thought it was funny at first, but soon  they grew tired of the constant expulsion of gas. But Barry just kept on burping. He simply couldn't help it.

It was lunchtime, so Mrs. Frightenright's class made their daily journey to the cafeteria. Barry nervously ate his lunch, hoping he wouldn't burp and make the other kids sick to their stomachs. It wasn't his fault that the cafeteria was serving pizza, chili, macaroni and cheese, and spicy bean burritos for lunch. Barry couldn't help eating two portions of each and washing it down with a bucket of extra-fizzy soda.

Lunchtime was soon over, and Barry sat back on his bench satisfied. He was relieved that he had not burped during the entire meal. The other kids were quite pleased about the nonburpage factor, too. But, unfortunately, they were still pretty upset because they had just heard the news from the cafeteria lady that the cafeteria had run out of desserts. It was announced that the plane that was supposed to deliver desserts to school was running late so the kids wouldn't get their goodies that day.

Barry wasn't thrilled that his meal wouldn't be finished off with a yummy snack. But his attention was quickly diverted . . . Barry's eyes crossed as he suddenly felt the biggest burp in his life brewing inside his stomach. His eyes watered. "This one is going to be dangerous!" Barry said as the burp continued to grow in his stomach like no other burp before it. He covered his mouth with both hands and thought ungassy thoughts.

Barry realized that there would be no stopping this burp. He knew that the magnitude of this burp would be lethal, so he ran as far away from the cafeteria as he could. Barry got to the far end of the playground when Big Bully Bob stopped him.

"Where are you going so fast, Barry?" Big Bully Bob asked.

Barry didn't answer; he just stood there with both hands over his mouth.

Big Bully Bob yelled, "Answer me when I'm talking to you!" Big Bully Bob grabbed Barry's hands and pulled them off his mouth.

It was then that the biggest burp in the history of mankind was released. Big Bully Bob was blown to another city.

The burp's force tipped an airplane that was flying overhead. The plane, intended for the International Dessert Delivery Station in Topeka, Kansas, just happened to be carrying the desserts for every school in the United States of America! The cargo dropped out of a door in back of the plane and landed with an explosion right in the middle of the playground. Double-Messy-Macro-Chocolate Bars With Nuts flew all over the place.(A few boxes without nuts were also found for the kids who preferred the nutless variety.) The rest of the class was just getting out of the cafeteria for recess when they all cheered.

"DESSERT!!!"

The kids grabbed two and three Double-Messy-Macro-Chocolate Bars apiece! Big Mouth Moira shouted, "Hooray for Barry! If it wasn't for his burps we would never have gotten this much dessert!"

Barry smiled because he had the new proud title of "The Burpingest Hero of All Time."

READING

Mrs. Frightenright asked, "Well, how was everybody's lunch?"

Jared rubbed his protruding belly and said, "One thing is for sure. It was the best dessert I ever had!"

Mrs. Frightenright said, "Good, now that we have enjoyed our midday nourish-

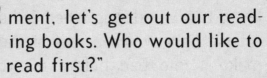

ment, let's get out our reading books. Who would like to read first?"

In a flash, Skip quickly shot his hand into the air. Skip was fast. I mean, when you look up "fast" in the dictionary, there's a picture of Skip. When he ran from one side of the house to the other, he looked like a blur. Before most kids woke up, Skip had mowed the lawn, swept the floors, walked and fed the dogs, and delivered the whole city's newspapers.

One night, Skip

lay in bed wondering whether he could turn off the light switch across his bedroom and make it into bed before the room turned dark. The next night, Skip got up and decided to try. He knew this meant running at the speed of light. Skip ran so fast that he ran around the whole world in less than a second. He ran straight across the oceans and everything!

He didn't just run at the speed of light, he went *F   A   S   T   E R!* When Skip stopped running, the year was 2150. This proved one of Einstein's theories, that if someone goes faster than the speed of light, time will slow down and they will be able to travel into the future. Skip thought that the future was weird! Robots were everywhere and people just sat around eating jelly donuts all day. Most robots just sat around, too, making the jelly donuts for people to eat all day.

Skip didn't know anybody because all of his friends were in the past. And he never much cared for jelly donuts. Skip didn't like the future, so he ran backward faster than

the speed of light until he came back to the present day. Skip still ran fast, but never **THAT** fast again.

Mrs. Frightenright called on Skip to read, so he stood up behind his desk, cleared his voice, and concentrated. The class saw Skip's lips vibrate as they heard a high-pitched squeal coming from his general direction. Then Skip sat back down in his seat. Mrs. Frightenright asked, "Well, Skip, are you going to start reading any time soon?"

Skip said, "I just read the entire book out loud."

"That was very fast," Mrs. Frightenright commented.

"Yes, ma'am, I'm very fast," Skip replied.

"Thank you very much, Skip. Now we can move on to art," Mrs. Frightenright said as the class put their reading books away.

ART

Carla Medulla was the world's smartest kid. The other kids could ask her any question and she would know the answer. Weird Ellis once asked her, "Carla, what's two hundred and fifty-seven times ninety-three?"

Carla Medulla answered, "Twenty-three thousand nine hundred and one." Mrs. Frightenright pulled out her calculator to see if Carla was correct. "That is absolutely amazing, Carla!" Mrs. Frightenright said.

Carla could learn almost anything, but the problem was she couldn't draw. Heck, she could barely even trace. But the worst part of it was she refused to learn how to draw. Mrs. Frightenright said, "Carla, it is very good that you are so smart, but you need to round yourself out by at least *trying* to draw."

Carla said, "I am the smartest kid in the world. I do not need to draw!"

The truth of the matter was that Carla was afraid of failure. Art was the only subject where she was receiving low grades. Mrs. Frightenright was a perceptive teacher so she went to Carla Medulla's desk and spread out a clean sheet of paper on her desktop. Mrs. Frightenright said, "I'll show you how to draw a funny cat!"

Within a few minutes, Carla was drawing the funny cat. "I can draw!" she exclaimed. "I drew this cat! That was so easy that I'll draw another one!" she said. Carla kept Mrs. Frightenright's instruction sheet in her pocket for the rest of her life.

Do you want to see the piece of paper Mrs. Frightenright made for Carla? Well, here it is! Now you can draw a funny cat, too . . .

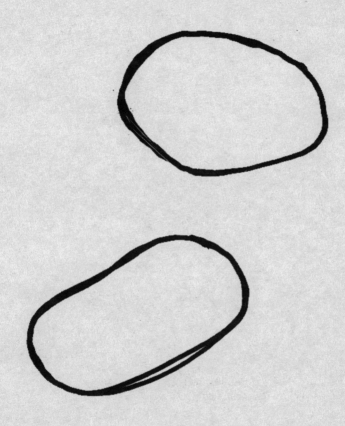

step one

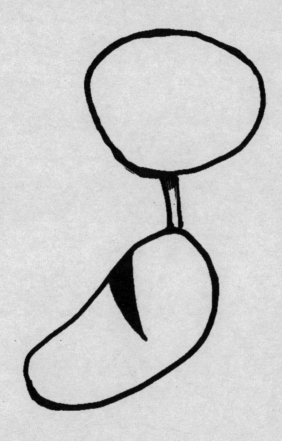

step two

step three

step four

MATHEMATICS

It was time for math and Sander Salamander had worked all night on his homework. Sander was a great big salamander with shiny black and red skin. He liked math and would have been thoroughly enjoying his math lesson

48

if it wasn't for the fact that his distant cousins were trapped in an aquarium right beside him in the classroom.  Sander just could not concentrate on Mrs. Frightenright's exciting math lecture as long as his pals were stuck in captivity.

He jumped up on his desk and yelled,

"This is so unfair! Here we are in America, 'The Land of the Free,' yet my cousins sit in a tank here against their will! This is a crisis of epic proportion and I'm not just gonna sit here and watch it happen!"

Mrs. Frightenright said, "Now, Sander, you need to calm down!"

Sander was spitting a lot when he talked.

"No way! Man, this is proof that the system is trying to cage all of us salamanders! Oh, first we're just your pets and the next thing you know we'll be on your dinner plates!"

Big Mouth Moira crinkled her nose. "Gross! I don't want to eat a salamander! I wouldn't be caught dead eating a salamander!"

Jared turned to Moira and said, "Hey, you big liar! I just saw you eat two salamanders yesterday."

"Oh, yeah," Moira said.

Mrs. Frightenright tried to calm Sander. "If it is so important to you, go ahead and let them go."

Sander grabbed the fish tank full of salamanders and lifted it. "Come on, fellas. I'm gonna let you go free in the stream!"

One of the salamanders looked up at Sander and screamed, "Hey, buddy! We don't want to go back to the stream!"

"Yeah!" said another salamander. "When I lived in the water, it was so full of pollution that I was sick all the time. And when we got out of the water and climbed onto the riverbank, some mean old cat would be waiting there, trying to eat us!" He pulled a little hanky out and dabbed his tear-filled eyes.

Sander was embarrassed. "I'm sorry, fellas, I just didn't think — "

"That's right, you didn't think!" another salamander interrupted. "Do YOU want to live in the river?"

"No," Sander said.

"Neither do we, so put our tank back where you found it!" the first salamander said.

Sander lifted the tank onto the table. He carefully scooted it back to where it was before. Sander pulled out his own handkerchief and dabbed the sweat from his forehead. Sander crawled back to his chair and listened quietly to the rest of Mrs. Frightenright's lecture.

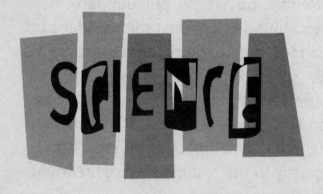

SCIENCE

When math was over Mrs. Frightenright said, "I have a special friend that I brought with me today!" The class looked puzzled. They didn't remember seeing anybody new in the classroom.

Mrs. Frightenright asked,

"Can anyone see something that is in the class-room today that wasn't in the classroom yes-terday?"

Mikey Mold asked,

"Is it Doug O'Dork's brain?"

Doug O'Dork turned red in the face and yelled at Mikey,

"Hey, wisenheimer! I think the huge booger hanging out of Mikey's nose wasn't here yesterday!"

Mikey yelled,

"What the heck is wisenheimer supposed to mean?! That's a stupid name!"

Doug yelled back,

"I know it's stupid, just like you!"

Mrs. Frightenright said, "Now, boys, that's quite enough! Doesn't anyone see the ten-foot-tall box in the corner?"

Everybody turned and saw a giant wooden crate standing in the corner. Mrs. Frightenright whistled and then yelled, "You can come out now, Clubber!"

The box burst open and a huge kangaroo wearing boxing gloves stood tall. His ears were enormous and he wore a bandage on a scab on his nose. Mrs. Frightenright

warned the class, "Clubber is a real pussycat . . . until he gets surprised, so don't make any sudden moves!"

Ellis asked, "Can we pet him?"

"Yes, you may," Mrs. Frightenright said.

Wet Willis asked, "Can we put a dress on him?"

"Uh . . . no," Mrs. Frightenright said.

The whole class stood up at once, which totally shocked Clubber. The kangaroo instantly started punching the air! He turned and punched a hole through the chalkboard!

Mrs. Frightenright yelled,

"Everyone sit back down immediately!"

"Everyone sit back down immediately!"

The class sat down in their seats.

After Clubber looked as if he had thrown his last punch and had calmed down considerably, Mrs. Frightenright suggested, "I think we should all pet Clubber one at a time. Ellis, you may go first."

Weird Ellis slowly walked up to Clubber. The kangaroo was about nine feet tall. He was, after all, a heavyweight boxing champion. Ellis petted Clubber on the belly and felt his soft, tan fur. Clubber began purring and lowered one of his boxing gloves, gently holding it out to Ellis.

Mrs. Frightenright said, "I've had Clubber as a pet now for ten years and he's never offered to shake someone's hand! He must really trust you, Ellis!"

Ellis and Clubber shook hands. Ellis said,

"It's too bad we can't get Principal Prickly-Pear in the boxing ring with you. It would be a total knockout!"

Just then the door flew open and Principal Prickly-Pear came in shouting. Clubber looked surprised and the next thing the class knew, Principal Prickly-Pear was lying on the ground with stars flying all around his head. Clubber had gotten excited and knocked him out cold! Mrs. Frightenright helped Principal Prickly-Pear up and walked him to the nurse's office, where he got a tetanus shot in the rear.

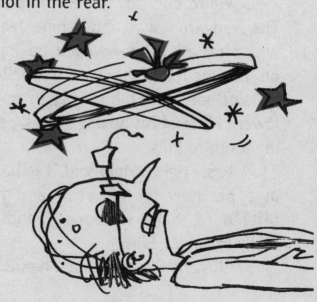

While Mrs. Frightenright was gone, the kids played with Clubber. Peter Darch sat in the kangaroo's pouch. Clubber hopped around the classroom until Peter got sick.

"My turn! I'm next!" Flying Vera screamed. "I want to get sick next!"

"Forget it, Vera. I'm going next!" Barry burped.

"No, me!" bubbled Wet Willis.

Clubber was so tired of hearing the children bicker that he went back into his big wooden crate and slammed the door shut. The children looked at each other.

SLAMM!!

"Touchy," Doug said.

Jared the pig was

upset that he didn't get to ride the kangaroo. Jared crossed his hooves and yelled,

"RIP-OFF!
I never get to do anything!"

Mrs. Frightenright returned to the classroom and saw that Clubber was back in his wooden crate. "Somebody must have upset poor Clubber," Mrs. Frightenright said.

Wet Willis apologized. "I'm sorry, Mrs. Frightenright. I think I was being a little selfish."

Flying Vera added, "We were all pretty pushy."

Mrs. Frightenright said, "I see that you learned your lesson. I happen to know that Clubber will come out of the box if you lure him out with his favorite food."

"What's his favorite food?" Weird Ellis asked.

"Dog food?" Moira guessed.

"Meat?" Peter asked.

"Small kangaroos?" Clockboy hypothesized.

Mrs. Frightenright pulled a corn dog out of her purse. The class heard Clubber sniffing from inside the giant crate. He broke the door down and hopped over five rows of desks in one leap to be next to Mrs. Frightenright.

"Here you go, Clubber," Mrs. Frightenright said as she fed him a corn dog.

The kids patiently took turns petting Clubber as he ate his corn dog.

Mikey Mold said, "It looks like we learned a lot today."

"I learned how to share," Moira said.

"I learned how to take turns so a kangaroo won't go back in a box," Wet Willis said.

Weird Ellis added, "I learned how to turn my eyelids inside out."

DISMISSAL

Mrs. Frightenright dismissed her students. The kids streamed out of the classroom, as Principal Prickly-Pear oozed in. Mrs. Frightenright was looking at her schedule. "Tomorrow is Friday . . ." she said, ". . . and that means that Clockboy will visit us from Tuesday. Oh, and I must remember to bring some extra mealworms to feed the salamanders."

"So, Mrs. Frightenright!" Principal Prickly-Pear yelled, holding an ice pack to his black eye.

"OH! You startled me. I didn't see you sneak in," Mrs. Frightenright said.

"This class thinks you're so cool!" he sneered.

"I guess so, Principal Prickly-Pear. I'm sure they think you're pretty cool, too," Mrs. Frightenright said.

"No, Mrs. Frightenright. They all laugh at me in the hallway as I pass. They like to say that I stink, and they call me wiener!" he hissed.

Mrs. Frightenright tried to encourage him. "I'm sure some of the students like you."

"It doesn't matter, Mrs. Frightenright!" Principal Prickly-Pear said. "You see, I am going to fix you and each and every one of your crazy little kids tomorrow!"

"Then we'll see who's so cool!"
he replied as he tripped over the doorstop

on his way out of the room.

Beware, for tomorrow is

Friday!

Well, reader, tomorrow is Friday. That's the last day of the week! Tomorrow will be the most exciting day yet! Secrets will be revealed! And we will finally find out what that Principal Prickly-Pear is up to. Here's a sneak peek from Mrs. Frightenright's tomorrow . . .

See

you in

class tomorrow!